Australian Shepherds

by Grace Hansen

Abdo Kids Jumbo is an Imprint of Abdo Kids
abdobooks.com

abdobooks.com

Published by Abdo Kids, a division of ABDO, P.O. Box 398166, Minneapolis, Minnesota 55439.
Copyright © 2022 by Abdo Consulting Group, Inc. International copyrights reserved in all countries.
No part of this book may be reproduced in any form without written permission from the publisher.
Abdo Kids Jumbo™ is a trademark and logo of Abdo Kids.

Printed in the United States of America, North Mankato, Minnesota.

052021

092021

Photo Credits: Alamy, iStock, Shutterstock, Thinkstock

Production Contributors: Teddy Borth, Jennie Forsberg, Grace Hansen
Design Contributors: Dorothy Toth, Pakou Moua

Library of Congress Control Number: 2020947647

Publisher's Cataloging-in-Publication Data

Names: Hansen, Grace, author.

Title: Australian shepherds / by Grace Hansen

Description: Minneapolis, Minnesota : Abdo Kids, 2022 | Series: Dogs | Includes online resources and
    index.

Identifiers: ISBN 9781098205997 (lib. bdg.) | ISBN 9781098206550 (ebook) | ISBN 9781098206833
    (Read-to-Me ebook)

Subjects: LCSH: Sheep dogs--Juvenile literature. | Herding dogs--Juvenile literature. | Dogs--Juvenile
    literature. | Animal behavior--Juvenile literature.

Classification: DDC 599.772--dc23

Table of Contents

Australian Shepherds

In the 1800s, **Basque shepherds** came to the United States from Australia. They brought dogs with them. These dogs later became the Australian shepherd **breed**.

Australian shepherds began as skilled farm and ranch dogs. Today, Aussies also work as guide and **therapy dogs**. Others are police or rescue dogs.

SERVICE DOG
IN TRAINING
DO NOT TOUCH

Aussies are medium-sized dogs.

They have strong legs and

muscular bodies.

9

Aussies have long, wavy or straight hair. They come in many beautiful colors.

Aussies can be black, red, or blueish in color. Some have a **merle** coat pattern. They may also have white or tan markings.

An Aussie's eyes can be brown,
blue, or amber. Some Aussies
have two different colored eyes.
One eye can also have specks
of different colors.

Grooming

Aussies need to be brushed weekly. This will keep their coats healthy. It will also help with **shedding**.

Exercise

Aussies can live in the city but are happiest with a large yard. They need lots of exercise. Once they are done growing, they make great jogging buddies.

Personality

Aussies are wonderful family pets. They are smart, easy to train, and loyal. Besides love and care, they need a job to do!

More Facts

- Many Australian shepherds still herd cattle today in the American West.

- A healthy Australian shepherd can live for 12 to 15 years.

- Australian shepherds belong to the herding group of dog **breeds**. This means they have the ability to control the movement of other animals.

Glossary

Basque shepherd – a person known for expert shepherding from the borderlands between France and Spain. In the early 1800s, many Basques travelled to Australia with their dogs to herd sheep, and later sailed to California where ranchers were introduced to their amazing dogs.

breed – a particular type of animal.

loyal – showing devotion and faithfulness to someone.

merle – a coat pattern that creates patches of color.

shed – to give off hair.

therapy dog – a dog that goes with its owner to visit people in order to bring comfort or cheer. Therapy dogs are different from service dogs, which are specially trained to perform specific tasks.

Index

Visit **abdokids.com** to access crafts, games, videos, and more!